Pebble® Plus
Bilingüe/ Bilingual

Exploremos la galaxia/Exploring the Galaxy
Los astronautas/Astronauts

por/by Thomas K. Adamson

Traducción/Translation: Dr. Martín Luis Guzmán Ferrer

Editor Consultor/Consulting Editor: Dra. Gail Saunders-Smith

Consultor/Consultant: Dr. Roger D. Launius
Chair, Division of Space History
National Air and Space Museum
Smithsonian Institution, Washington, D.C.

Capstone press®
Mankato, Minnesota

Pebble Plus is published by Capstone Press,
151 Good Counsel Drive, P.O. Box 669, Mankato, Minnesota 56002.
www.capstonepub.com

Library of Congress Cataloging-in-Publication Data
Adamson, Thomas K., 1970–
    [Astronauts. Spanish & English]
    Los astronautas / por Thomas K. Adamson = Astronauts / by Thomas K. Adamson.
    p. cm. — (Pebble plus, exploremos la galaxia = Pebble plus, exploring the galaxy)
    Includes index.
    ISBN-13: 978-1-4296-0065-1 (hardcover)
    ISBN-10: 1-4296-0065-9 (hardcover)
    1. Astronautics — Juvenile literature. 2. Outer space — Exploration — Juvenile literature. I. Title. II. Title: Astronauts.
III. Series.
TL793.A2818 2008
629.45 — dc22   2007003493

Summary: Simple text and photographs describe astronauts — in both English and Spanish.

Editorial Credits
Katy Kudela, bilingual editor; Eida del Risco, Spanish copy editor; Kia Adams, set designer; Mary Bode, book designer;
    Jo Miller, photo researcher/photo editor

Photo Credits
Corbis Sygma/Jacques Tiziou, 19
Digital Vision, 4–5
NASA, 1, 6–7, 9, 11, 13, 15 (both), 21
Photodisc, cover, 17

Note to Parents and Teachers

The Exploremos la galaxia/Exploring the Galaxy set supports national science standards related to earth science. This book describes and illustrates los astronautas/astronauts in both English and Spanish. The photographs support early readers in understanding the text. The repetition of words and phrases helps early readers learn new words. This book also introduces early readers to subject-specific vocabulary words, which are defined in the Glossary section. Early readers may need assistance to read some words and to use the Table of Contents, Glossary, Internet Sites, and Index sections of the book.

Table of Contents

Tabla de contenidos

Astronauts

Blast off!

A space shuttle leaves Earth.

A crew of astronauts

is on its way to space.

Los astronautas

¡Despegamos!

El transportador espacial

abandona la Tierra.

La tripulación de astronautas

va rumbo al espacio.

Astronauts are part
of space missions.
They risk their lives
to learn more about
the solar system.

Los astronautas son parte
de las misiones espaciales.
Ellos arriesgan su vida
para aprender más sobre
el sistema solar.

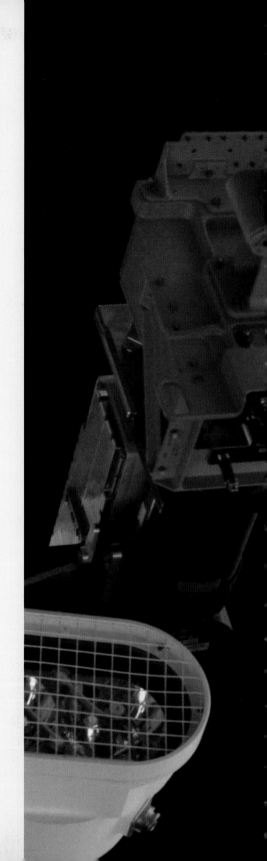

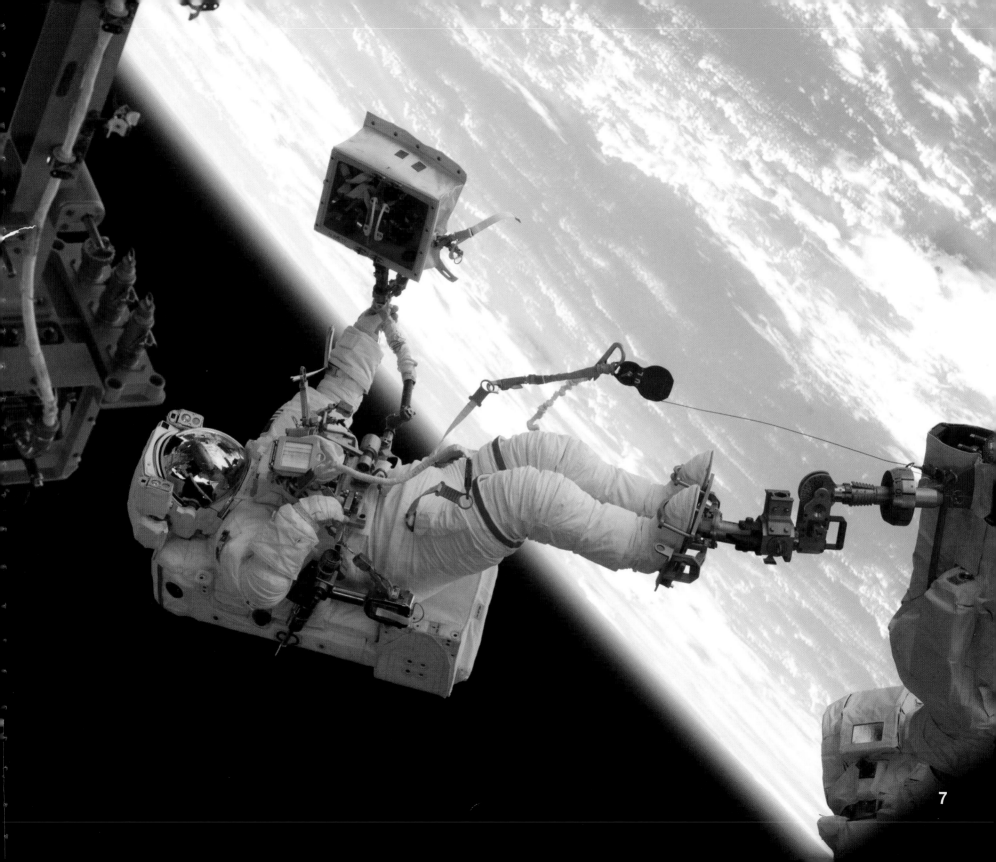

Astronauts at Work

Astronauts have jobs

to do in space.

They do tests.

They fix satellites.

El trabajo de los astronautas

Los astronautas tienen labores

que hacer en el espacio.

Hacen pruebas.

Arreglan los satélites.

Astronauts can work
outside of their ships.
They go on space walks.

Los astronautas pueden trabajar
fuera de sus naves. Pueden hacer
caminatas espaciales.

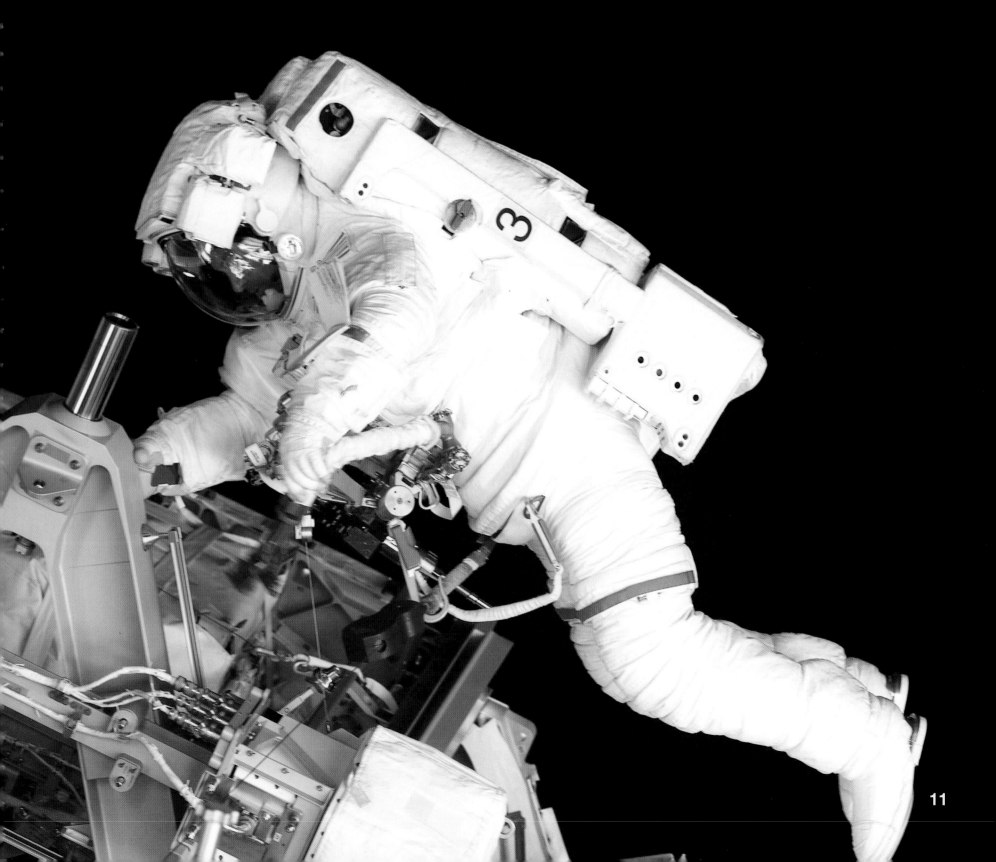

There is no air in space.

Astronauts wear space suits

so they can breathe.

En el espacio no hay aire.

Los astronautas usan trajes

espaciales para poder respirar.

Some astronauts live
and work on space stations.
They can stay in space
for months at a time.

Algunos astronautas viven y
trabajan en estaciones espaciales.
A veces se quedan en el espacio
durante varios meses.

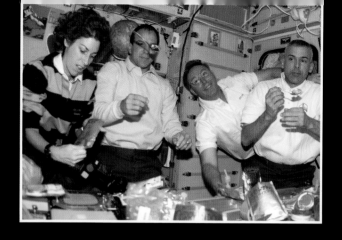

Exploring Space

Astronauts explore space

like no one else can.

They float above Earth.

They can walk on the Moon.

Explorando el espacio

Los astronautas exploran el espacio

como sólo ellos pueden hacerlo.

Flotan sobre la Tierra.

Pueden caminar en la Luna.

Astronauts have landed
on the Moon six times.
They studied the Moon.
They gathered rocks and soil.

Los astronautas han llegado
a la Luna seis veces. Así han
estudiado la Luna. Ahí han
recogido piedras y tierra.

Astronauts will keep

exploring space.

What do you think

they will learn

on their next mission?

Los astronautas van a continuar

explorando el espacio.

¿Qué crees que puedan

aprender en su próxima misión?

Glossary

crew — a team of people who work together

mission — a group of people who are sent to do a special job

satellite — a spacecraft that takes pictures and sends messages to Earth

solar system — the Sun and the objects that move around it; our solar system has eight planets, dwarf planets including Pluto, and many moons, asteroids, and comets.

space shuttle — a spacecraft that carries astronauts into space and back to Earth

space station — a spacecraft that circles Earth; astronauts can live on space stations for long periods of time.

space walk — a period of time during which an astronaut leaves the spacecraft to move around in space

Glosario

la caminata espacial — lapso de tiempo durante el cual un astronauta deja la nave espacial para moverse en el espacio

la estación espacial — nave espacial que da vueltas alrededor de la Tierra; los astronautas pueden vivir en las estaciones espaciales durante periodos largos de tiempo.

la misión — grupo de personas enviadas a hacer un trabajo especial

el satélite — nave espacial que toma fotos y envía mensajes a la Tierra

el sistema solar — el Sol y los objetos que se mueven a su alrededor; nuestro sistema solar tiene ocho planetas, planetas enanos, incluyendo a Plutón, y muchas lunas, asteroides y cometas.

el transportador espacial — nave espacial que lleva a los astronautas al espacio y los regresa a la Tierra

la tripulación — equipo de personas que trabajan juntas

Internet Sites

FactHound offers a safe, fun way to find Internet sites related to this book. All of the sites on FactHound have been researched by our staff.

Here's how:

1. Visit *www.facthound.com*

2. Choose your grade level.

3. Type in this book ID **1429600659** for age-appropriate sites. You may also browse subjects by clicking on letters, or by clicking on pictures and words.

4. Click on the **Fetch It** button.

FactHound will fetch the best sites for you!

Sitios de Internet

FactHound te brinda una manera divertida y segura de encontrar sitios de Internet relacionados con este libro. Hemos investigado todos los sitios de FactHound. Es posible que algunos sitios no estén en español.

Se hace así:

1. Visita *www.facthound.com*

2. Elige tu grado escolar.

3. Introduce este código especial **1429600659** para ver sitios apropiados a tu edad, o usa una palabra relacionada con este libro para hacer una búsqueda general.

4. Haz un clic en el botón **Fetch It**.

¡FactHound buscará los mejores sitios para ti!

Index

Índice